D1503246

Sherlick Hound and the Valentine Mystery

Kelly Goldman and Ronnie Davidson

Pictures by Don Madden

Albert Whitman and Company
Niles, Illinois

Text © 1989 by Kelly Goldman and Ronnie Davidson
Illustrations © 1989 by Don Madden
Published in 1989 by Albert Whitman & Company,
5747 West Howard Street, Niles, Illinois, 60648
Published simultaneously in Canada
by General Publishing, Limited, Toronto
All rights reserved. Printed in U.S.A.
10 9 8 7 6 5 4 3 2 1

Library of Congress Cataloging-in-Publication Data

Goldman, Kelly.
   Sherlick Hound and the valentine mystery/Kelly Goldman and
Ronnie Davidson; illustrated by Don Madden.
         p.   cm.
   Summary: When Princess Penelope Poodle's ruby collar is stolen at
her Valentine's Day party, detective Sherlick Hound doggedly checks
out Dogtown's high society until he finds the thief.
   ISBN 0-8075-7335-3
   [1. Mystery and detective stories. 2. Dogs—Fiction.]
I. Davidson, Ronnie. II. Madden, Don, 1927-   ill. III. Title.
PZ7.G5685Sh 1989   88-20561
[E]—dc19   CIP
                                                        AC

To Louis, Steve, Jill, Alexis, and Max—
staunch "Digger" supporters. K.G. and R.D.

Sherlick Hound leaned back in his chair, his hind feet propped up on his desk, a milkbone clenched in his teeth. Business had been slow lately, and Sherlick, the Dog-Honest Detective, was anxious for some action.

BR-R-R-R-I-N-G!

Sherlick jumped up and grabbed the phone.
"Dog-Honest Detective Agency, Sherlick here," he
barked into the receiver.

"Hello, Sherlick darling," a voice crooned on the
other end.

Sherlick sighed and leaned back again. It was only
his old friend Princess Penelope Poodle.

"Hello, Princess," said Sherlick. "What can I do for you today?"

"I'm going to do something for *you*, darling," said Penelope. "I'm inviting you to my Valentine's Day party. It's Saturday on the *Red River Queen*. Everydog who's anydog will be there, you know. Bye, now."

"Well, that's no mystery," said Sherlick, hanging up the phone. "But it will be good for a free cup of chow."

On Saturday, the *Red River Queen* sparkled with the jewels of Dogtown's high society. Everyone was there—wealthy businessman Sir Archibald Airedale and his wife, Princess Penelope Poodle; Lola Lhapso, hairdresser to the stars; the world-famous opera star

Tosca Terrier and her agent, Monty Mongrel; and
jewelry designer Gloria Vanderdog. Helping out were
Chef Chow and Sailor Spaniel.

Valentine hearts were everywhere, for Sir Archibald
wanted Penelope to have a perfect Valentine's Day.

Sherlick and his friend Scoop Schnauzer, roving reporter, were the last to arrive. The paddle on the *Red River Queen* began to turn, and the boat set off downstream.

"Great setting for a crime," said Scoop.

"One I could sink my teeth into," answered Sherlick.

"Anything for excitement, old dog," said Scoop. "Things have been awfully quiet lately. I could use a good story."

In the ballroom, Sir Archibald Airedale was about to
make a toast.

"Dear friends," he began. "Let's drink to my wife,
Princess Penelope." He handed her a glass of punch.
"Happy Valentine's Day, sweetheart," he said.

"Oh, Archie," Penelope squealed. "What is this in my glass?"

"A beautiful ruby collar for a beautiful princess," he said. "Designed by the talented Gloria Vanderdog."

Sir Archibald wiped off the collar and put it around Penelope's neck.

"Oh, Archie, it's grand," said Penelope. "And you know red is my favorite color."

As everyone admired Penelope's gift, the lights went
out. There was crashing and banging and howling.

"What's going on?" Sir Archibald yelped.

"Where's the switch?"

"Help! You're standing on my tail!"

"Here's the switch!" And the lights came on.

"My collar is gone!" screamed Penelope. "My beautiful ruby collar is missing!"

"It's been stolen!" shouted Sir Archibald. "There's a thief aboard!"

"There's no thief, Sir Archibald," Gloria's voice soothed. "Here's the collar. It fell on the floor. You probably just didn't fasten the clasp tightly," she continued. "Let me do it." Gloria put the collar around Penelope's neck.

"Thank goodness, Gloria," said Penelope.

"Too bad," Scoop Schnauzer whispered to Sherlick. "That had the smell of a good story."

"We could all use a breath of fresh air," said Sir Archibald, leading the guests up the stairs. "I'm sure I fastened that collar properly," he muttered as everyone walked out on deck.

Suddenly, a wave rocked the boat, throwing Gloria and Penelope off balance. They flipped over the rail and fell into the water.

"Help! Help!" shouted Gloria. "I can't swim!"

"To the rescue!" Sherlick called. He dove overboard and pulled Gloria and Penelope to safety.

"Oh, thank you, Sherlick," said Penelope. "You saved our lives—and my collar!" She raised her paw to feel her new gift.

"What's this?" exclaimed Sherlick. "Are you hurt?"

"I don't think so," said Penelope.

"Your neck is bleeding," said Sherlick.

Penelope looked at her paw. It was covered with red.

"Let me see that collar," Sherlick said.

Penelope unhooked the collar and gave it to Sherlick.

"This collar is glass colored with red paint, and the paint is running," said Sherlick. "When Sir Archibald gave you the collar in a glass of punch, it didn't run. This is not the same collar," Sherlick declared. "Princess Penelope, I'm afraid this collar is a fake!"

"Then someone *has* stolen my collar," said Penelope. "But who could it be?"

"It seems we have a mystery, after all," Sherlick said. He winked at his friend Scoop Schnauzer.

"Happy Valentine's Day, Princess Penelope!"
announced Chef Chow, wheeling in a five-tiered,
heart-shaped valentine cake.

"Dig the paws on Chef Chow!" whispered Scoop.
"They're all red!"

"Right," said Sherlick. "We'd better keep an eye on
him." He took a pad and pencil from his inside pocket
and began to jot down notes.

Sherlick strolled over to where Gloria was eating her cake. "Do you usually eat with your gloves on, Gloria?" he asked.

"Of course, dear," she answered. "A lady *always* wears gloves."

Sherlick smiled as he pictured Gloria in a bathtub with her gloves on.

"Look over there," said Sherlick. "Isn't that Lola Lhapso, hairdresser to the stars?"

"Sure is," said Scoop.

"And look at her paws," said Sherlick.

"RRRRed," growled Scoop.

"Better keep an eye on her, too, Scoop," said Sherlick.

"No problem!" said Scoop, licking his chops. "Whatever Lola wants, Lola gets!" He made his way over to where Lola was standing.

Out of the corner of his keen detective's eye, Sherlick spied splotches of red paint on the deck.

"Now where could these lead?" he wondered, following the trail. It led to an open doorway. Sherlick peered into the dark room.

"Anyone here?" he called.

Sailor Spaniel stepped out. "Only me, Mate," he replied.

"What's going on in there?" Sherlick asked.

"Nothing to worry about, Mate," said Sailor Spaniel. Sherlick noticed that Sailor Spaniel was splattered with red paint. Scratching thoughtfully behind his ear, Sherlick wrote another note in his pad.

Scoop poked his head around the corner. "Dig up anything?" he asked.

"Just a few old bones," replied Sherlick.

"Well, I've got a bone for you to chew," said Scoop. "Lola let it slip that Sir Archie's company is losing money—lots of it!"

"Good work, Scoop," said Sherlick. "Keep sniffing around."

Then Sherlick spotted Tosca Terrier, world-famous opera singer, howling at the moon. She was decked out in jewels from head to tail.

"Great-looking rocks, Tosca," said Sherlick. "You're really loaded down."

"Oh, yes," Tosca said. "I'm a soft touch when it comes to jewelry. When I see something I like, I just *have* to have it."

Monty Mongrel swaggered up, nudging Sherlick aside. "Is this clue sniffer bothering you, Tosca, baby?" he growled. He took Tosca's paw. "Let's dance!" Tosca and Monty tangoed off together.

"Two worthy suspects," Sherlick said, scribbling their names in his pad.

Sherlick stood deep in thought, gnawing on his milkbone. Then, smiling to himself, he disappeared into the ship's radio room.

When he came out, Sherlick bumped into Sir Archibald. "Archie," said Sherlick, tearing a page from his notebook and handing it to Sir Archibald, "I want you to gather everyone on this list in the captain's cabin. And please be there yourself."

"Certainly, Sherlick," said Sir Archibald. "Do you know who the thief is?"

"We'll see," answered Sherlick.

When Sherlick entered the captain's cabin, Sir Archibald, Princess Penelope, Scoop Schnauzer, Gloria Vanderdog, Chef Chow, Tosca Terrier, Monty Mongrel, Sailor Spaniel, and Lola Lhapso were waiting anxiously.

Sherlick looked at each one in turn.

"The thief who stole Princess Penelope's ruby collar is in this room," he announced finally.

Everyone gasped and looked around.

Princess Penelope
Scoop Schnauzer
Gloria Vanderdog
Chef Chow
Tosca Terrier
Monty Mongrel
Sailor Spaniel
Lola Lhapso

"You, Chef Chow," said Sherlick. "You have red stains on your paws. You could have stolen the collar."

"Oh, no!" said Chef Chow. "Those stains are from the red food coloring I used to make Princess Penelope's valentine cake."

"You, Sailor Spaniel," said Sherlick. "You're covered with red spots! You look like a Dalmatian with measles. You could have stolen the collar."

"No, sir, Mate," said Sailor Spaniel. "I got this red on me from touching up the paint on this old boat."

"Tosca," continued Sherlick, "you and Monty are a perfect team. It's obvious you love jewelry. While Monty turned off the lights, you could have switched the collars."

"Why, Sherlick," protested Tosca. "I'd never do such a thing. Penelope is my best friend!"

"Tell him the truth, baby," said Monty, yanking a strand of pearls from Tosca's neck. "These are all fakes!"

"Why, who would have guessed!" cried Penelope.

"I'd never waste my money on the real thing," said Tosca. "Real jewelry is no fun. You have to keep it in the bank vault or someone might steal it."

"Then there's Lola," said Sherlick. "Look at these paws!" He held up Lola's red paws.

"I just did a dye job on Poo Poo Pomeranian this morning," she said. "But she'll kill me if you breathe a word that she dyes her fur!"

"As for you, Sir Archibald," said Sherlick. "There's no red on you, but rumor has it your company is in the red. You could have stolen the collar to cash in on the insurance and save your business."

Sir Archibald laughed. "I started that rumor myself! Someone was buying up all my stock, and I wanted to stop them."

"All the guests have shown their paw except you," said Sherlick, pointing at Gloria Vanderdog. Reaching over, he pulled off her glove. There were red stains all over her paw. "Why is *your* paw all red, Gloria?" Sherlick accused.

Gloria twisted out of his grasp and ran from the room.

While everyone chased after Gloria, Sherlick took a milkbone out of his pocket and put it in his mouth. He walked out on deck and leaned against the rail, waiting.

Scoop Schnauzer ran up, panting. "Why aren't you trying to catch Gloria?" he asked Sherlick.

"How far can she go?" answered Sherlick. "We're on a boat in the middle of the water, and Gloria can't swim!"

Scoop laughed. "You're a clever dog," he said.

Just then, Gloria raced around the corner. Sherlick stuck out his hind leg and tripped her. Gloria went sprawling across the deck. Her hat flew off, and the ruby collar tumbled out.

"Well, well," said Sherlick. "What have we here?" He picked up the ruby collar and rubbed it against his coat sleeve. "Seems to be the real thing," he said.

Sherlick looked down at Gloria, lying in a heap on the deck.

"For once I wanted some real jewels," Gloria sobbed. "I work with real jewels. I create gorgeous jewelry. But I can never afford any of my own!"

At that moment, the Harbor Patrol boat pulled alongside the *Red River Queen*. Inspector Doberman climbed aboard. "Detective Hound, you radioed that you had a theft," said the Inspector. "Can you use some help?"

"Everything's under control, Inspector," said Sherlick. "We caught our jewel thief red-handed. Take her away."

Sherlick put the ruby collar around Princess Penelope's neck.

"This will make headlines!" exclaimed Scoop.

"Oh, thank you for getting my collar back, Sherlick," said Penelope. "But how did you know Gloria was the thief?"

"Gloria herself said, 'A lady *always* wears gloves,'" explained Sherlick. "However, Gloria wasn't wearing gloves until *after* the valentine collar was stolen. The paint on the phony collar must have been wet when Gloria switched the collars, so she had to put her gloves on to hide her red paws."

"Good job, old chap," said Sir Archibald. "You're an amazing detective."

Scoop chuckled. "*That's* no news," he said. "Sherlick Hound, Dog-Honest Detective, always solves his case!"